To Princess Eliza Esmé Haynes

K. L.

To all at Arena with thanks for their support

S. H.

Bloomsbury Publishing, London, New Delhi, New York and Sydney
First published in Great Britain in 2014 by Bloomsbury Publishing Plc
50 Bedford Square, London, WC1B 3DP

Text copyright © Kate Lum 2014
Illustrations copyright © Sue Hellard 2014
The moral rights of the author and illustrator have been asserted

A CIP catalogue record of this book is available from the British Library

ISBN 978 1 4088 2425 2

Printed in China by C&C Offset Printing Co Ltd, Shenzhen, Guangdong

1 3 5 7 9 10 8 6 4 2

www.bloomsbury.com

Princesses Are Not Just Pretty

Kate Lum

Illustrated by Sue Hellard

BLOOMSBURY

LONDON NEW DELHI NEW YORK SYDNEY

Once there were three princesses:
Princess Allie, Princess Mellie and Princess Libby.
They lived in a palace by the sea.
There was **always** so much to do in the Princessdom,
and the princesses were **always** very busy.

Now, they were having a well-earned rest under the rose trellis.
"Good work today," said Allie, taking her third cupcake.
"Yup, excellent princess-ness, all round," agreed Libby, as she sipped her tea.

"The good thing is," added Mellie, "we work so hard, and we still look fabulous. I know **I'm** the prettiest, but **you** two look great, as well!"

Allie and Libby stared at each other. Then they stared at Mellie. "What do you mean, you're the prettiest?" demanded Allie.

"Oh, nothing," said Mellie, "it's just that, I am. Well, someone has to be the prettiest," said Mellie, peering at her reflection in the teapot, "and it happens to be me."

"Actually," sniffed Princess Libby, "I am the prettiest. It's no good denying it. It's my nose, you see – the way it pokes up at the end is just adorable."

"Sorry," interrupted Allie, "but I am the prettiest. It's my freckles, the way they sprinkle my cheeks, like cinnamon. Everyone loves cinnamon!"

"As I was saying before I was interrupted," said Mellie, "I am the prettiest. It isn't everyone who has purple hair, you know. It's extra special."

"I am the prettiest," said Allie sharply.

"I am the prettiest," insisted Libby.

"I told you three times, I am the prettiest!" cried Mellie.

Mrs Blue arrived to clear the trays.

"Mrs Blue," shrieked all the princesses at once,

"which of us is the prettiest?"

"Oh, dear. Must rush along," said Mrs Blue.

"WHICH?" demanded the princesses.

"Oh, look, is that a squirrel?" asked Mrs Blue.

"We can't think about anything else until we solve this," said Mellie. "I know: let's have a **beauty contest!**"

"Oh, yes!" cried Allie and Libby at once.
"Oh, no!" said Mrs Blue.

And so it was decided. The beauty contest would take place that Saturday, and four of the cleverest girls in the land were picked to be the judges.

The day before the contest, Allie, Mellie and Libby rushed around, making themselves as pretty as possible.

Allie gave her hair a special treatment.

Libby bathed in beautifying goo.

Mellie tried on a few dresses.

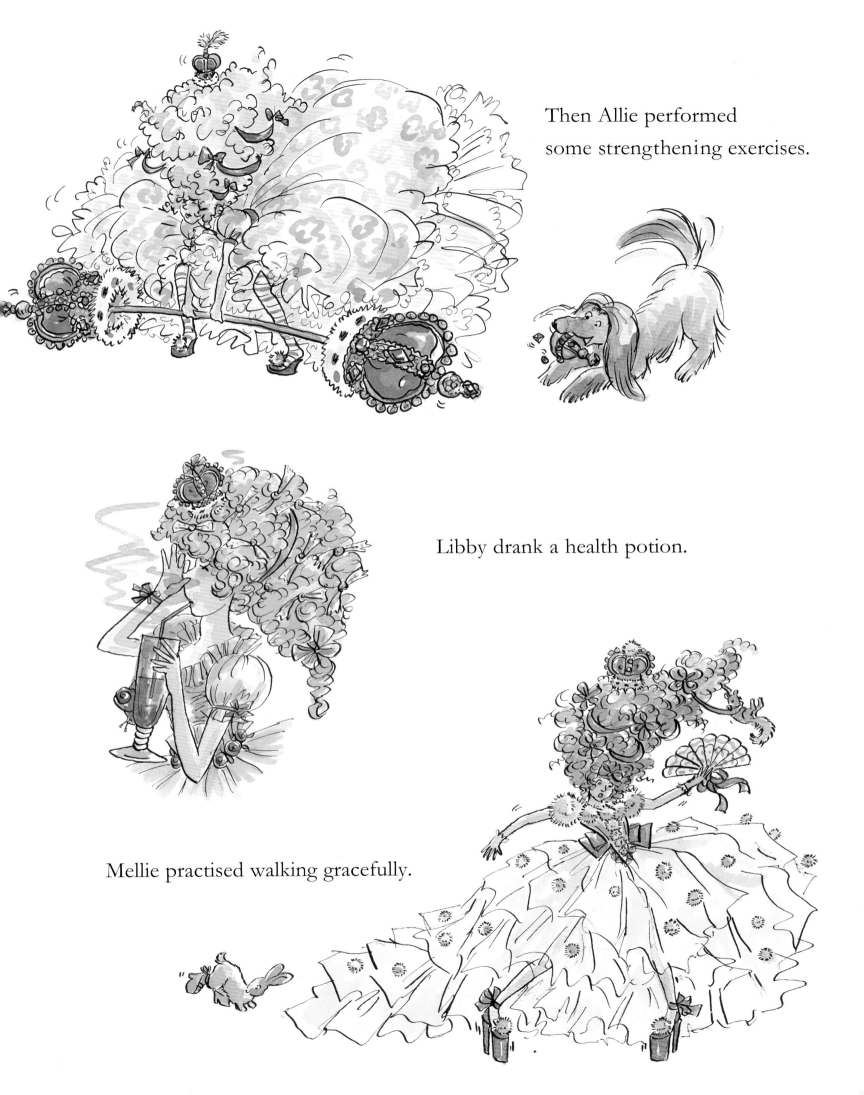

Then Allie performed
some strengthening exercises.

Libby drank a health potion.

Mellie practised walking gracefully.

Then . . .

Allie developed the perfect curtsey.

Libby tried out an elegant wave.

Mellie wrote a victory speech.

And . . .

Allie enhanced her freckles
with cinnamon.

Libby scrubbed her tilted nose.

Mellie curled her purple hair.

And they all went to bed and dreamed of being the prettiest.

Early the next morning, Princess Allie got up.
She put on her finest gown and set off
for the contest.

As she passed the Palace Bakery, however, she smelled something strange.
She poked her head inside and gasped – smoke!

Thick smoke was pouring from the ovens.

The servants had gone to see the contest, and forgotten the Royal Bread.

Allie grabbed a hose and sprang into action. **WHOOSH!**

Meanwhile, Libby put on her loveliest gown
and marched out, nose first, to the contest.
But, as she passed the park, she heard a sound.

"Help! Oh, no! Help meee!"
It was coming from the duck pond.

Libby raced over, just in
time to see a little girl wade
into the deep mud by the
side of the water.

"My kitty fell in!
He can't swim!"
cried the little girl.
"I can swim!" called Libby.
And she did.
SPLASH!

At the same time, Princess Mellie was ready for the contest. She strolled out, thinking her hair had never looked purpler. But, as she stepped along the lane, she heard a small voice shouting . . .

"Pigs! Pigs!
Get back here, pigs!
Pig alert! Waaaait!"

Past her feet ran a line of piglets,
followed by a very small boy
in a muddy shirt.

"Help, Princess!" he shouted.
"My pigs!"
And so, she helped. **SPLAT!**

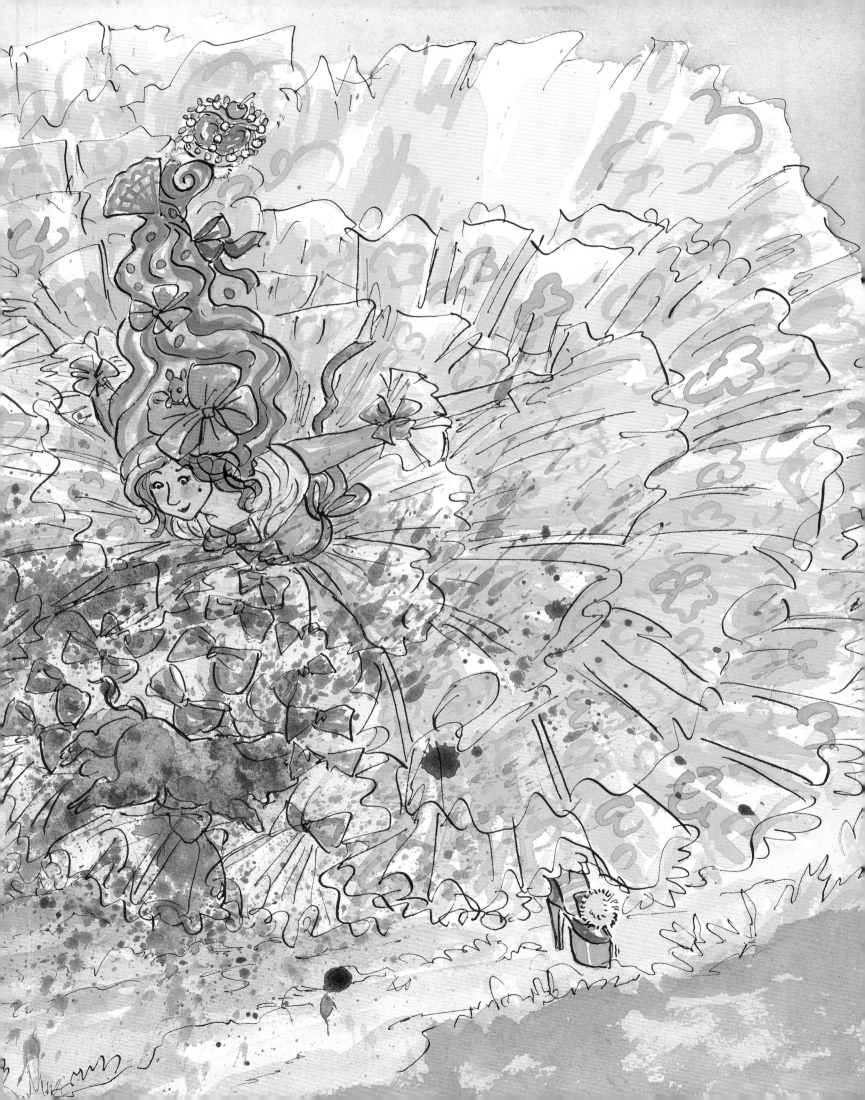

Meanwhile, at the contest hall, the people were getting restless.
Mrs Blue tried to help; she sang a few songs,
she played the accordion, she even performed a dance.
But where, oh where, were the princesses?

At last, the Royal Page blew his trumpet. "The princesses have arrived!" he announced.
The curtains parted, and all the people sat up, eager to see their Royal Prettinesses.

One by one, they stepped onto the
stage. Princess Allie came first.
She looked . . . remarkable.

Princess Libby came next.
She looked . . . incredible.

Princess Mellie came last.
She looked . . . unforgettable.

The audience whispered as the judges wrote on their score cards. At last, the smallest judge stood on her chair.

"We hereby announce our decision," she read. "Of all the princesses ever seen in the Land:

Princess Allie is:
the yuckiest!

Princess Libby is:
the drippiest!

And Princess Mellie is:
the muddiest!

You have **all** shown us
that **princesses are not just pretty!"**

"Three cheers for
the Best Princesses!"
cried all the people.